My
self-confidence diary
for girls

Your guide to accepting yourself as you are and overcoming your fears

Marguerite Depradel

My self-confidence diary for girls

© Marguerite Depradel

Self-confidence is an extraordinary power that resides within you, capable of transforming a simple thought into a powerful action. It drives you to make your voice heard, to pursue your dreams with determination, and to become the incredible person you're meant to be.

Yet sometimes there's that little negative voice that creeps into our minds. It whispers that you can't, that it's too hard, that it's too risky. But here, in these pages, we're going to confront that little voice and silence it.

This diary is designed to be your companion on this adventure. It will guide you through exercises, insights and activities that will help you develop your self-confidence and fully embrace your inner potential.

Ready to begin this incredible adventure? Let you become the confident version of the great person you already are.

Table of contents

"The doors of the future are open to those who know how to push them."

COLUCHE (COMIC)

"They didn't know it was impossible so they did it."

MARK TWAIN (WRITER)

you

Self-confidence means accepting yourself as you are. You can't please everyone or agree with everyone all the time. You have your opinions, your tastes, your qualities and flaws, your successes and setbacks, your personal background. These are the things that make you interesting and unique.

That doesn't mean you shouldn't improve what you can, or change what you don't like if you want to. It just means that you are you, and that's fine. You don't have to be perfect or always trying to please others or be accepted.

Accepting yourself as you are means knowing who you are, what you like and what you want for yourself, now and in the future. That's why, throughout this guide, you'll be able to answer questions about yourself that will help you get to know yourself better. There are no right or wrong answers. The important thing is to be honest with yourself.

What is self-confidence?

Circle the answers that seem right to you.

Speaking louder than other people in order to silence them

Speaking up to give your opinion when it's your turn

Doing only what you like

Boasting and belittling other people to make you feel better

Respecting yourself and the others

Making fun of other people

Taking advantage of other people' weaknesses

Setting your own limits

Being sassy or defying authority

Doing the activities you enjoy

Being yourself

Taking action to achieve your goals

Self-confidence

The correct answers appear in **bold** below. As you may have guessed, self-confidence does not mean defying authority or belittling others. It is self-assertion and self-respect while listening to and respecting the others. It is placing oneself on the same level as the others, neither below nor above.

Speaking louder than other people in order to silence them

Speaking up to give your opinion when it's your turn

Doing only what you like

Boasting and belittling other people to make you feel better

Respecting yourself and the others

Making fun of other people

Taking advantage of other people' weaknesses

Setting your own limits

Doing the activities you enjoy

Being sassy or defying authority

Being yourself

Taking action to achieve your goals

Are you feeling confident?

Why or why not? What does it mean on a daily basis? Think of concrete examples where you think you have or haven't shown self-confidence.

Let's think about it

Think of someone you know who seems to have confidence in themselves. It could be a friend, a family member or a celebrity.

What adjectives come to mind? You can write down other adjectives that seem appropriate to describe this self-confident person.

STRONG

BRAVE

BOLD

SMART

AWESOME

NICE

SPECIAL

FUNNY

BEAUTIFUL

GREAT

INDEPENDENT

PROUD

OPTIMIST

OPEN-MINDED

FRIENDLY

CALM

Your role models

It's important to recognize self-confidence in others, and it's not a bad idea to draw inspiration from them. Think of women, both famous and close to you, whom you admire for their self-confidence. How does their self-confidence express itself? Think of their voice, their gaze, their body language, for example.

(1) ___________________________________

____

____

(2) ___________________________________

____

____

(3) ___________________________________

____

____

(4) ___________________________________

____

____

____

(5) ___________________________________

____

____

Describe yourself

Now it's your turn! Circle the adjectives that best describe you. Add any other adjectives you think are appropriate.

STRONG	CREATIVE
BRAVE	COOL
BOLD	POPULAR
SMART	SPORTY
CALM	GENEROUS
TALENTED	SWEET
BEAUTIFUL	STYLISH
NICE	INDEPENDENT
FRIENDLY	OPTIMIST
FUNNY	BOUNCY

_____________________ _____________________

_____________________ _____________________

_____________________ _____________________

_____________________ _____________________

And the others?

Take the same list and circle the five adjectives you'd like people to think of when they see you. Do you think this is the case? You can also ask people you trust to give you three adjectives that describe you to them. Use different colors to circle the adjectives you'd like people to think of you as, and the answers from people you trust.

STRONG	CREATIVE
BRAVE	COOL
BOLD	POPULAR
SMART	SPORTY
CALM	GENEROUS
TALENTED	SWEET
BEAUTIFUL	STYLISH
NICE	INDEPENDENT
FRIENDLY	OPTIMIST
FUNNY	BOUNCY

_______________________   _______________________

_______________________   _______________________

_______________________   _______________________

Your areas of interest

If you were to write a book or make a movie, what would it be about?

____

____

If you could meet anyone in the world, who would it be?

____

What question would you ask him or her?

____

____

What subject(s) do you prefer studying?

____

____

If you could travel back in time, when would you go?

____

Which countries would you like to visit?

____

What three new things would you like to experience?

1 ______________________________________

2 ______________________________________

3 ______________________________________

What you enjoy doing

Circle your favorite activities and add the ones you can't find.

Playing an instrument or singing

Thinking about new things

Doing yoga

Building things

Doing sports

Dancing

Studying history

Doing scientific experiments

Leading others, organizing

Writing stories or articles

Teaching to others

Taking part in a show

Drawing, painting or sculpting

Hiking or being in the wilderness

Helping the others

Learning computer skills

Discussing or debating

Taking care of animals

Studying planets and space

Finding solutions to problems

Cooking

Discover your passions

Perhaps you don't yet know what you're passionate about... When we're growing up, it's essential to discover what motivates us. It's through our passions that we can express our creativity, develop our talents and find meaning in our lives.

A passion is an activity, subject or field that interests us deeply. It's something that thrills us, energizes us and gives us a sense of satisfaction and happiness. Passions can be varied: music, sport, reading, art, science, writing, cooking and so on. Everyone has their own passions, and it's important to discover and explore them.

- **Try out new activities**: Sign up for courses, take part in workshops, join clubs or associations. This will enable you to discover new areas and meet people with similar interests.

- **Make a list of what interests you**: Go back over the list of activities or subjects that thrill you. Write down any ideas that come to mind, even if they seem far-fetched.

- **Explore your talents**: You've already thought about what you do well, what you get compliments on. Your talents may be linked to your passions, and cultivating them will allow you to grow even more.

- **Be curious**: Ask questions, read books, watch documentaries, explore the Internet. The more you learn about different subjects, the more likely you are to discover what you're passionate about.

- **Listen to your heart**: When you're doing something you're passionate about, you'll feel a deep sense of joy and motivation. Listen to your emotions and follow your heart to discover your true passions.

Cultivate your talents and passions

Once you've identified your strengths, it's time to **cultivate and develop them**. Talents are like seeds that need watering and nurturing to grow. Think of ways to put your strengths into practice and improve them. For example, if you're good at drawing, you could take art classes to hone your skills. If you're good at math, you could enter competitions or help classmates who are struggling.

It's also important to **explore new activities** and get out of your comfort zone. Sometimes we discover hidden talents by trying something new. Try participating in clubs or workshops that interest you. You might be surprised at what you can do. To take the drawing example again, why not try a sculpture or writing class to develop your creativity? For math, a related activity might be learning to play chess or code.

Experimentation will enable you to discover new passions and develop new skills, while reinforcing those you already possess.

Here are a few tips to help you cultivate your passions:

- **Make time for your passions**: Set aside time in your diary for your favourite activities. Whether it's an hour a day or a few hours a week, the important thing is to make time for what you're passionate about.

- **Set yourself goals**: Set clear, achievable goals related to your passions. This will motivate you and help you measure your progress. For example, if you're passionate about music, set yourself the goal of learning to play a new instrument, play a difficult score or compose a melody.

- **Surround yourself with like-minded people**: Join communities, clubs or groups of people who share your passions. You'll meet inspiring people, share experiences and support each other in your development.

- **Experiment and explore**: Try new things, explore new areas related to your passions. This will help you discover new facets of your interests.

- **Be persistent**: Cultivating your passions takes time, effort and perseverance. Don't be discouraged by obstacles or difficulties. Keep practicing, learning and improving.

By exploring your passions and interests, you'll discover a side of yourself you may never have known existed.

What do you like about yourself?

There are probably aspects of your personality or look that you particularly like. Think about it for a moment and write down your main assets below:

1 ____

____

2 ____

____

3 ____

____

4 ____

____

5 ____

____

6 ____

____

7 ____

____

What are you good at?

There are certainly some subjects where you shine and some topics that you master better than many others. Think about it for a moment and write down your favourite subjects below.

1 ____

____

2 ____

____

3 ____

____

4 ____

____

5 ____

____

6 ____

____

7 ____

____

Your assertions

Think about everything that makes you unique and special and fill out these assertions in an honest and positive way. You don't have to answer all the questions at once.

I love who I am because…

____

____

I am good at…

____

____

I feel comfortable when…

____

____

What makes me laugh is…

____

____

I already succeeded in…

____

____

The place where I feel happy is…

I mean a lot to…

I am often praised for…

What energizes me is…

What I really like is…

I am gifted for…

Your positive board

Take all the positive statements and qualities you have identified in the previous pages and choose the ones you like the most, the ones you are most proud of. Write them down in your **positive board** on the next page. Choose beautiful colors and paste it so that you can see it on a regular basis. You can also paste pictures of you and the people you love, places or activities you enjoy the most. Feel free, it's your board!

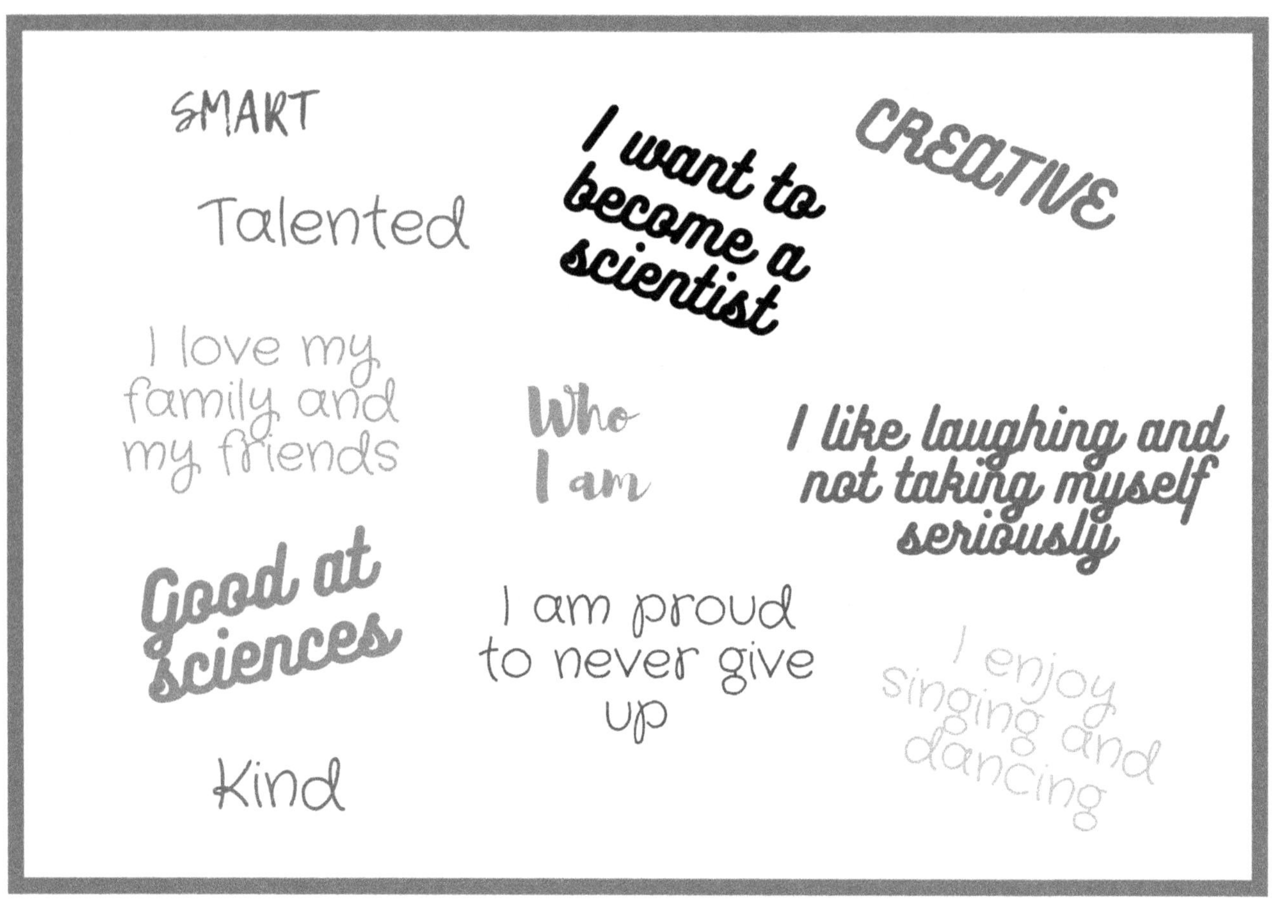

Who I am

Your rights

Complete this list if necessary. Read this manifesto aloud at least once a week and whenever you feel full of doubt or fear.

- I have the right to be respected.
- I have the right to set boundaries.
- I have the right to disagree.
- I don't always have to please others.
- I will speak up if someone makes me feel uncomfortable.
- No one can force me into doing something that goes against my values.
- No one can stop me from doing something I really care about.
- I am strong enough to accept the consequences of my choices and actions.
- I will seek help from a trusted adult if I need it.

Your rights

I have the right to…

feel sad

give my opinion

dislike things

NOT ALREADY KNOW IT ALL

be wrong

ask for help

ASK WHY

disagree

express my feelings

NOT TO BE LIKE THE OTHERS

CHANGE MY MIND

"Be yourself.
Everyone else is already taken."

OSCAR WILDE (WRITER)

"I'm convinced that about half
of what separates the successful
entrepreneurs from the
non-successful ones is pure
perseverance."

STEVE JOBS (ENTREPRENEUR)

Having confidence in yourself **means taking action**. Action could be talking to that nice looking group of girls or signing up for that singing activity you've been dreaming of. It could be signing up for soccer when no other girl is signed up, or it could be entering that mental math competition with math whizzes.

It's a lack of self-confidence that makes you wait until all the conditions are in place, not to take the risk of failing, being rejected or looking ridiculous. But are you sure that's what would happen? And if it did happen, would it be so bad?

We've already seen who you are. Now we'll see what you want. Think about everything you'd like to do. It could be something you can do tomorrow such as raising your hand in class, in a few months such as participating in a show, or in a few years such as becoming a karate champion.

Your goals

Think about what you would like to achieve. It could be short-term, like making a new friend, medium-term, like improving your grades in science by the end of the term, or long-term, like becoming an astronaut.

My goals are…

I know I can achieve them because I…

Your challenges

Think of something you dream of doing but have never dared to try. Imagine and write down the worst that can happen if you fail:

____

____

____

____

____

____

Now, do the same thing and imagine what would happen if you were successful.

____

____

____

____

____

____

____

Note below some **small daily challenges**. Don't set the bar too high. Aim for things you know you can do but often hesitate to do (say hello? smile? raise your hand in class? talk to others?) Colour in the box when you've successfully met your challenge. You can do it!

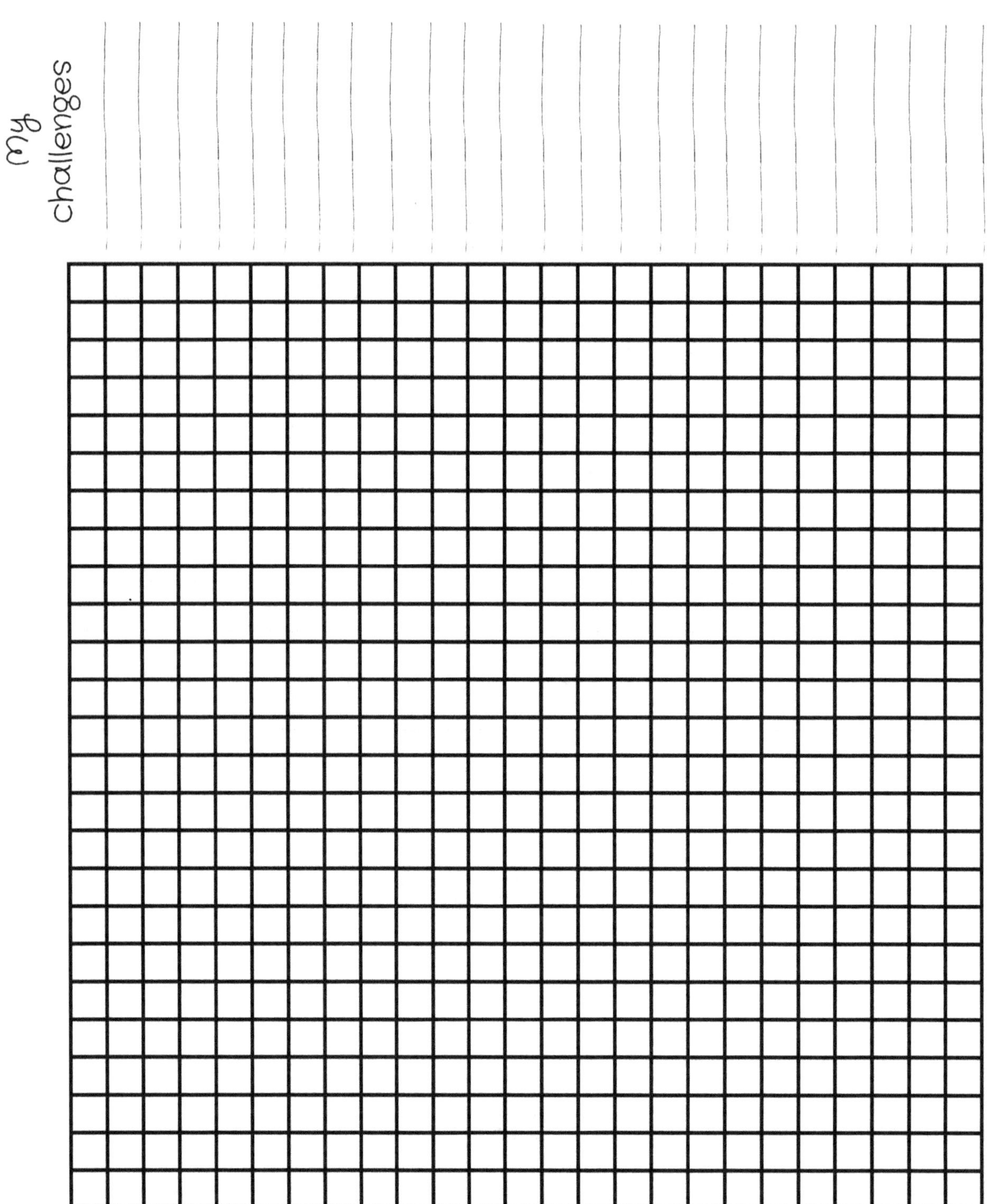

Setting long-term goals

Setting long-term goals is an important step towards growing in confidence and realizing your dreams. When you have clear goals, it gives you a direction to follow and motivates you to work hard to achieve them.

Set your goals

The first step in setting long-term goals is to define them clearly. Take time to think about what you want to achieve in your life. What are your dreams and aspirations? What are you passionate about? What areas do you want to improve in?

Once you've identified your goals, write them down. Write them down in a precise and detailed way. For example, instead of writing "I want to be rich", you could write "I want to become an entrepreneur and create a successful business in the field of technology".

Plan your actions

Once you've defined your goals, it's important to plan the actions needed to achieve them. Break down your long-term goals into short-term ones, and create an action plan for each step.

For example, if your long-term goal is to become a doctor, your short-term goals could be to be as good a student as possible, take reinforced science courses and volunteer at a hospital.

Plan the actions you need to take for each short-term goal and set yourself realistic deadlines.

Stay motivated

Setting long-term goals can sometimes seem daunting, especially when the results aren't immediate. It's important to stay motivated and keep your end goal in mind.

Find sources of inspiration that remind you why you set these goals. Read biographies of successful people in your field of interest. Surround yourself with positive, encouraging people who believe in you and your abilities.

Overcoming obstacles

On the road to achieving your long-term goals, you're likely to encounter obstacles and challenges. It's important not to give up and to find ways of overcoming them. Identify potential obstacles that may arise, and think of ways to overcome them.

Reassess and adjust

It's important to regularly reassess your long-term goals and adjust them if necessary. Life is constantly evolving, and it's normal for your goals to change over time.

Objective number __

My objective: _________________________________

____

I want to achieve this goal cause: _________________

____

My deadline: _____________

Step 1

Step 2

Step 3

Step 4

Obstacles

Answers

If _________________________

____

____

____

____

Then _________________________

____

____

____

____

Objective number __

My objective: _______________________________
____

I want to achieve this goal cause: _______________
____

My deadline: _______________

Step 1

Step 2

Step 3

Step 4

Obstacles   Answers

If _______________   Then _______________
_______________   _______________
_______________   _______________
_______________   _______________
_______________   _______________

Your dream board

Visualization can help to project yourself and make your goals more concrete. If your motivation is waning, take a look at your board. Paste inspiring photos of what you want to achieve on the next page or create your own format. You can type "dream board" or "visualization board" in Google or Pinterest to find more examples.

What I want

Take action

Action is a habit to take. The hardest thing is always to start. Here are a few tips to help you take action. For example, think about what you could change around you.

Things that can be improved in my classroom, my school, my street, my neighborhood are:

☆ ______________________________

____

☆ ______________________________

____

☆ ______________________________

____

☆ ______________________________

____

____

I want to change things because: ______________

____

____

____

____

____

____

____

Your plan to make a difference

1 Describe a problem you are facing:

____

____

____

____

2 Here are different ways to solve this problem:

☆ ____

____

☆ ____

____

☆ ____

____

☆ ____

____

☆ ____

____

3 Consider what could happen for each of the solutions listed above.

4 Circle the chosen solution. Use the next page to break down the actions you need to take.

Your plan to make a difference

4 The solution I chose:

____

____

____

The different steps to take action:

☆ _____________________________

____

☆ _____________________________

____

☆ _____________________________

____

☆ _____________________________

____

☆ _____________________________

____

Remember that you can always ask a friend or a trusted adult for help because together you are stronger. This means that with several people, you can often do more than you can on your own.

Get involved

Another way to take action is to **find a cause that motivates you** and for which you can work. Think about what you would like to change in society. This could be related to the environment, education, poverty, animal welfare, gender equality, for example. There are surely associations around you that need help. Maybe you can even suggest your class to organize an action to distribute useful information on this subject or to raise funds.

The causes that motivate me are:

Your plan to support the cause you've chosen

You can't save the world on your own. On the other hand, a single person of good will can achieve great things. You can do this by taking small steps.

Let's say you're at the beach and you notice some dirt on the sand or in the sea. What's your reaction? Leave it where it is, waiting for someone else to pick it up because it's not your job? Or take the bull by the horns, pick them up and dispose of them in the appropriate garbage can?

If you choose the latter, not only will you be cleaning up the beach, but you'll also be preventing people from injuring themselves on potentially dangerous garbage (like glass, for example) and marine animals from feeding on it.

With a bit of luck, you'll set an example for others to come and help you, or at least avoid littering in the future.

If you want to help a particular cause, think about all the little things you can do on your own. Then think about how you can create emulators (= people seeking to match or surpass your beneficial actions).

The following page will help you do just that.

Your plan to support the cause you have chosen

The cause I have chosen:

____

____

____

____

My ideas for action:

☆ __________________________________

____

____

☆ __________________________________

____

____

☆ __________________________________

____

____

☆ __________________________________

____

____

☆ __________________________________

____

____

Your plan to support the cause you have chosen

The quick wins I can easily achieve:

____

____

____

____

How I can convince other people to help me or do what I do:

☆ ____

____

____

☆ ____

____

____

☆ ____

____

____

☆ ____

____

☆ ____

____

____

Your plan to support the cause you have chosen

Write down your daily good deeds (or actions) and think of the good you spread around you.

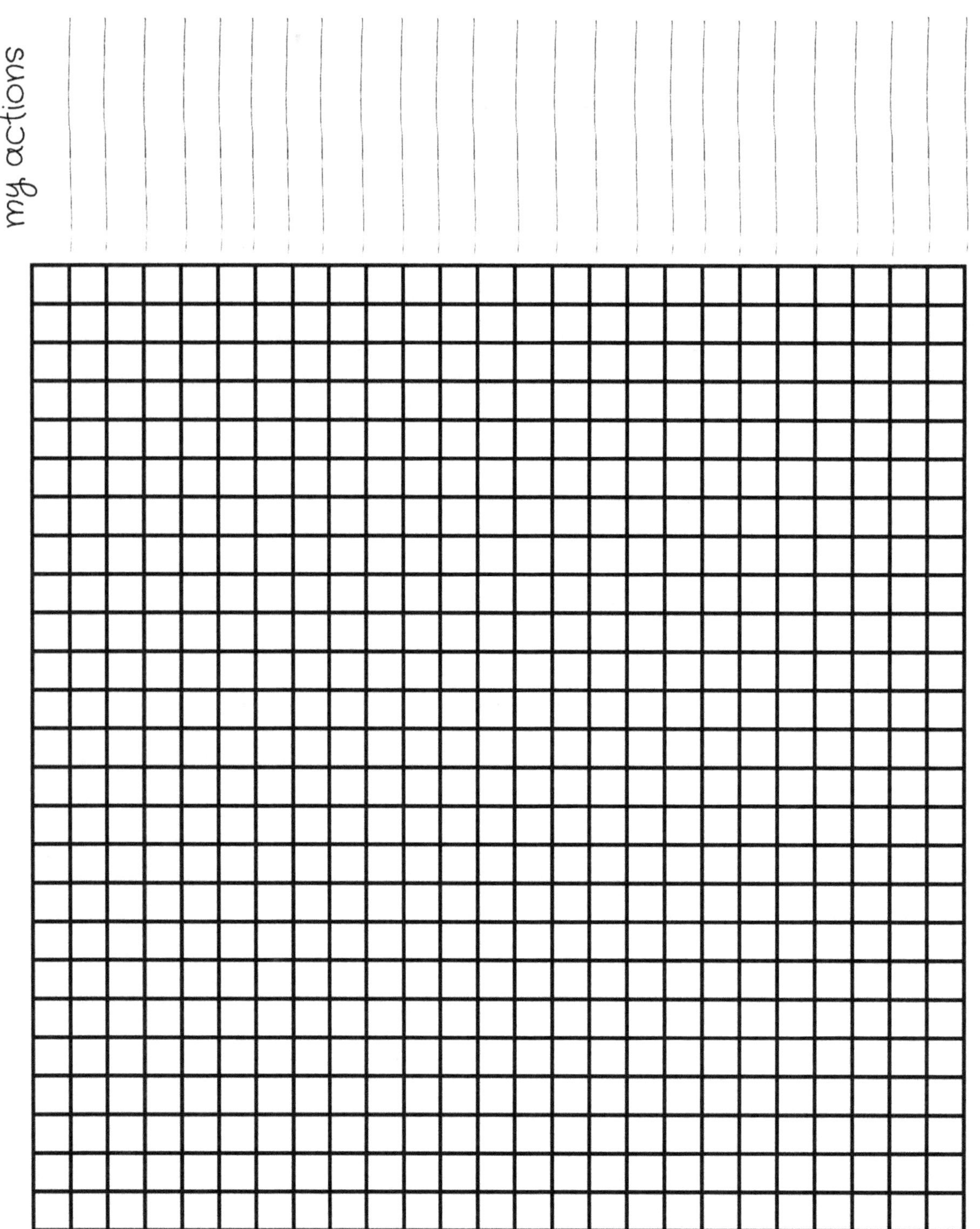

"No one can make you feel inferior
without your consent."

ELEANOR ROOSEVELT (AMERICAN
FIRST LADY)

"I did not fail. I simply found 10,000
solutions that don't work."

THOMAS EDISON (INVENTOR)

your achievements

To increase your self-confidence, you need to take off the negative glasses you sometimes look at yourself with. You can be your worst enemy without meaning to, by doubting more than necessary or criticizing yourself too harshly.

Think about all the great things you've already accomplished. Remember all the happy times you've had, all the people who care about you, all the people you love and admire.

You've thought about who you are and what you want. It's time to spend some time on why you should be proud - your accomplishments, big and small.

Your grounds for pride

List the moments when you felt proud of yourself. It could be a difficult test you passed, a contest you did well in, a race you won, a complicated choreography you mastered, a compliment you received, a joke that made your friends laugh.

1

2

3

4

5

Yes, there are several pages because you are great and your accomplishments are not going to stop there. Take a small notebook to keep track of all the things that make you proud. Keep it filled and read it over regularly.

(6) ______________________________

____

____

____

(7) ______________________________

____

____

____

(8) ______________________________

____

____

____

(9) ______________________________

____

____

____

(10) ______________________________

____

____

____

Stick pictures of moments or grounds of pride

Positions of power

Superwoman

Stand up and think of a time in your life when you felt proud of yourself. Now, with your feet apart, put your hands on your hips, lift your chin, shoulders back and chest out. Stand up straight as if a thread is pulling you up. Hold the position for two minutes.

Eagle

Standing, feet slightly apart, back straight, lift up your chin, shoulders back and chest bulging, spread your arms as if you wanted to push the walls. Hold the position for two minutes.

What you have just practiced are **positions of power**. Practicing them before an event you are concerned about gives you an extra dose of confidence.

Celebrate your wins!

There are no small victories. Are you happy and proud to have gotten a good grade or to have made someone smile? Enjoy the moment and invent a **gesture of celebration**. It could be a little dance or just raising your arms. Describe your gesture, take a picture or draw it. This will anchor the victory even more deeply within you.

List the times and places where you feel the most calm and happy

What are your thoughts during these moments? How are you feeling?

Smile

Paste below a picture of you at a particularly happy moment. Remember the place, the atmosphere of the moment, the sounds, the smells and your feelings. Are you smiling as you recall this memory?

Express your gratitude

Knowing how to appreciate what you already have is essential to being fulfilled. Saying thank you to life, to the people you love will make you happier and more confident.

In the evening, when you are quiet in your room, think about your day. Did you learn anything interesting? Did you laugh with your friends? Did you see or hear anything that you liked or were moved by? Did someone help you, compliment you, or just show that they liked you? Did you try something new?

You can keep a small notebook of all the things you are thankful for on a daily basis. If you keep a journal, you can also write them down every day. This will help you see life more positively and build your self-confidence.

I am thankful

For ____

____

For ____

____

For ____

____

For ____

____

For ____

____

For ____

____

____

____

____

"Life is not easy for any of us. But what of that? We must have perseverance and above all confidence in ourselves. We must believe that we are gifted for something and that this thing must be attained."

MARIE CURIE (PHYSICIST, NOBEL
PRIZE IN CHEMISTRY)

Taking risks

There are different types of risks. The risks that are worth taking, and the others. The only ones worth taking are the ones that bring something to you.

You may be more or less afraid of three types of risk:
- the risk of hurting yourself physically,
- the risk to show you as you really are,
- the risk of not being up to the task.

Everybody is afraid of something and it's completely natural. But you have to overcome your fears in order to act. Identifying the risks that are holding you back, visualizing what might happen if you took those risks, breaking them down into smaller risks, cheering yourself up, are all ways to overcome your fears and take useful risks. You can do it!

Risks

There are useful risks, which bring you something positive when you take them, and unnecessary risks that can get you into trouble. Do you know what the "right" risks are?

Talking to a stranger on the street

Giving out personal information online

Order a new dish at the restaurant

Performing a solo at the school's end-of-year show

Not studying for a major test in order to play longer

Try temporary hair color

Going out with a group of new friends after school

Coming home late without telling your parents

Joining a debate club

Going alone for a walk without telling anyone

Cheating at a test

Telling friends that you disagree with them

Taking the hardest route in sport

Talking to a new student at your school

Risks

Being confident doesn't mean taking any risks. It means taking smart risks (in black). It can be scary, but you know in your heart that these risks can bring adventure and joy into your life.

Talking to a stranger on the street

Giving out personal information online

Order a new dish at the restaurant

Performing a solo at the school's end-of-year show

Not studying for a major test in order to play longer

Try temporary hair color

Going out with a group of new friends after school

Coming home late without telling your parents

Joining a debate club

Going alone for a walk without telling anyone

Cheating at a test

Telling friends that you disagree with them

Taking the hardest route in sport

Talking to a new student at your school

Make a list of smart risks you would like to take. Then circle the one you would like to take the most:

What are the three things you're afraid might happen if you take this risk?

1

2

3

How could you reduce the possibility of failure?

By training? By convincing a friend to take this risk with you? By asking for advice from those around you? By breaking down the risk you'd like to take into smaller risks?

How could you break down the risk you would like to take into smaller risks?

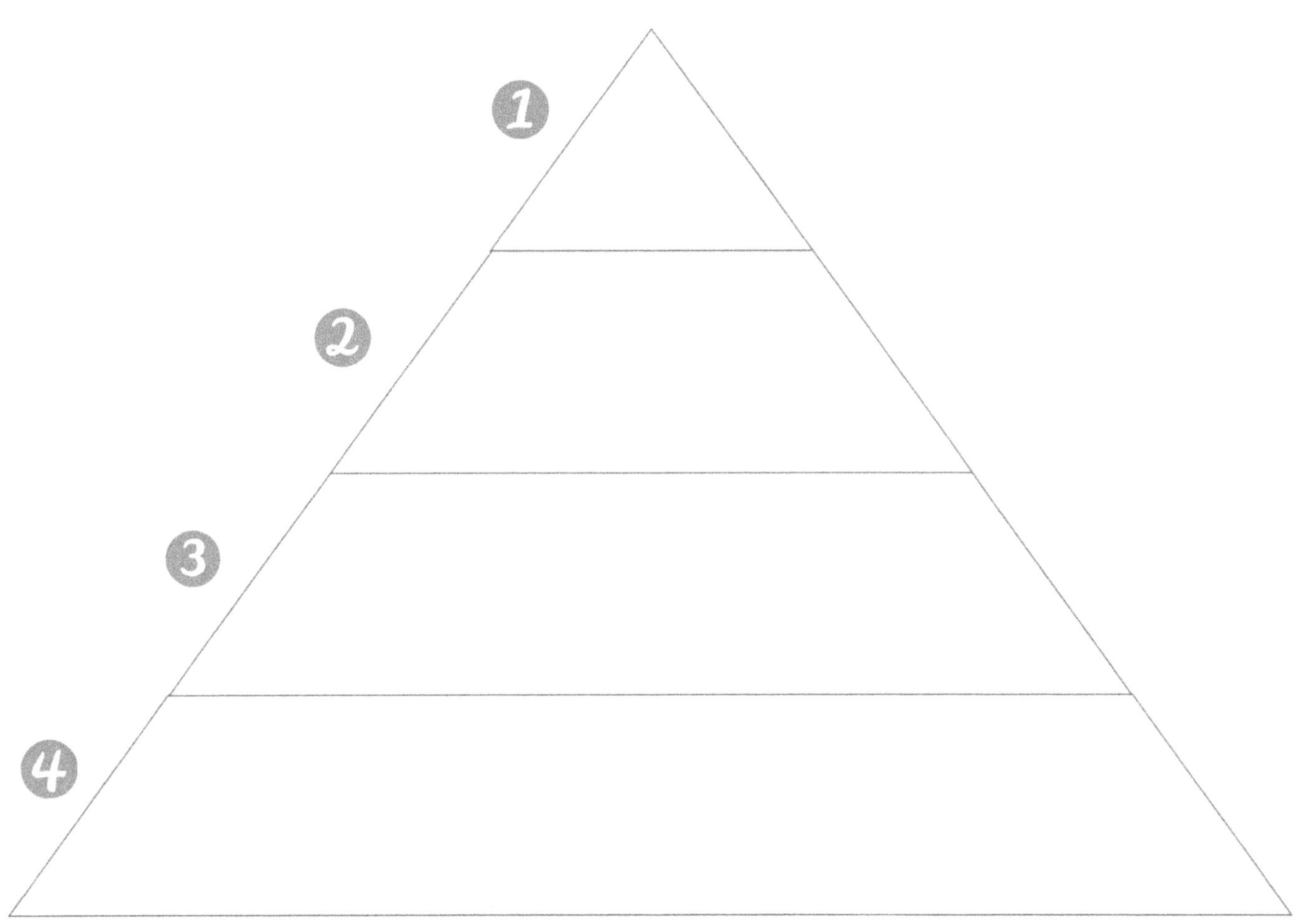

Now that you've broken down the risk you want to take into several smaller risks, implement step **①** of your plan.

Imagine what a tiny coach sitting on your shoulder could say to encourage you to take that risk:

Now imagine what the most confident person you know would say to you:

Your plan to take a useful risk

Colour in a box below every time you take a small, useful risk.
With practice, fear diminishes.

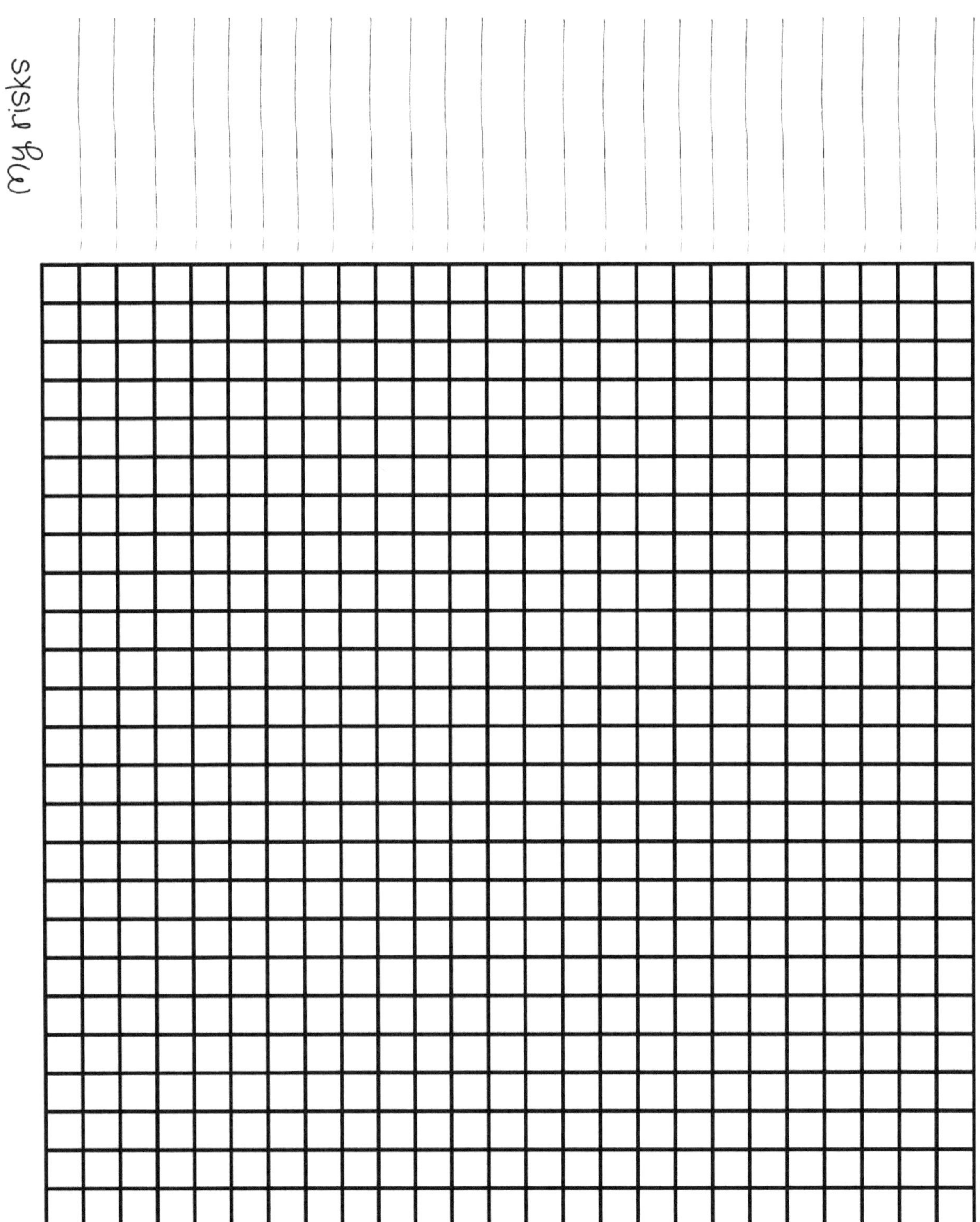

Let's go back to your first step. How did it go? Are there things you could improve? Carry on with your plan and assess each step:

Ask caring people around you, your parents, a teacher, a friend, to give you their recipe when they are having doubts about themselves:

What do they say to themselves? What do they imagine? You can also ask them to tell you about a time when they really doubted themselves, but were able to overcome their fear. Write down their answers below:

Now imagine what would happen if you never tried anything risky, if you only did things you already mastered.

What would you miss in your opinion? Would you lose out on interesting people or activities? Would you find it fun?

Dealing with other people's judgments

The judgment of others can be a source of stress and anxiety for many children and teenagers. It's natural to want to be accepted and appreciated by others, but it's essential to remember that the judgment of others does not define your self-worth.

Understanding the origin of other people's judgment
The judgment of others can come from a variety of sources, such as social pressure, cultural norms or family expectations. Other people's judgment is often a reflection of their own fears, insecurities and prejudices. By understanding this, you can begin to step back from other people's opinions and not let them affect you in a negative way.

Learning to distance yourself from the opinions of others
When you're concerned about the judgment of others, you tend to conform to their expectations and modify your behavior to be accepted. However, this can be exhausting and prevent you from being true to yourself. Learning to detach yourself from the gaze of others means being authentic and staying true to your values and convictions, even if it means being different from others.

It can be difficult, but by remembering that your self-worth doesn't depend on the approval of others, you can find the strength to stay true to yourself.

"A person who never made a mistake never tried anything new."

ALBERT EINSTEIN (SCIENTIST, NOBEL
PRIZE IN PHYSICS)

"Don't be afraid to make a mistake.
But make sure you don't make the same
mistake twice."

AKIO MORITA (MANUFACTURER)

Enemies

There are many enemies of your self-confidence:
- Perfectionism,
- Preconceived ideas about girls,
- False friendships,
- Harassment,
- Your negative thoughts,
- Your fears.

Some enemies are **external to you**, such as false friendships or harassment. Others are mixed, such as perfectionism, which may be yours or your parents', or preconceived ideas about girls, which are external at first, but which you may have unconsciously accepted.

Your negative thoughts and fears are your own. They are **internal enemies**. They arise from what you have experienced, seen and heard. They can thrive on small failures, negative remarks or experiences that you may have generalized. The factual "I missed a spin" becomes "I suck at gymnastics" and turns into a fear of doing sports.

The fears

Fears are natural emotions that we all feel at some point in our lives. They can be triggered by different situations or events, and can vary from one person to another. Understanding the origin of your fears is an important step towards overcoming them and developing your self-confidence.

Instinctive fears

Some fears are innate and part of our survival instinct. For example, the fear of danger, such as the fear of wild animals or the fear of falling from a great height. These fears are often present from an early age, and are important in protecting us.

Learned fears

Other fears are acquired over time, often through personal experience or external influences. For example, the fear of spiders can be learned if we have witnessed a fearful reaction in someone else. Similarly, fear of failure can be influenced by past experiences of difficulty or disappointment.

Irrational fears

Some fears may be irrational, i.e. without any real basis, such as the fear of clowns or enclosed spaces. These fears may seem disconcerting, but it's essential to remember that they are subjective and specific to each individual.

The influence of the environment

Our environment can also play a role in the development of our fears. If we grew up in an environment where fear was constantly present, this can have an impact on our own perception of fear. Similarly, if we've been exposed to scary stories, this can reinforce our fears.

Limiting beliefs

Our limiting beliefs can also contribute to our fears. For example, if we believe that we're not good enough or that we don't deserve success, this can create a fear of failure or a fear of judgment from others. It's essential to replace these beliefs with positive, encouraging thoughts.

The importance of introspection

To understand the origins of our fears, it's essential to practice introspection. Take the time to reflect on your fears and try to understand where they come from. Ask yourself questions such as:

- When did I start feeling this fear?
- Was there a specific event that triggered it?
- Is this fear based on real facts or suppositions?

Your fears

List the things you are most afraid to try and why. Are you afraid of getting hurt, of being laughed at, of having a bad result that will make you feel bad, of being judged as being different? Are these fears based on real facts?

1

2

3

4

5

Your fears

Here is a list of things that may seem scary. Circle the three that impress you the most. You can add more.

Post a picture of yourself online without a filter

Answering a question in class

Joining a group where you don't know anyone

Playing a new sport

Making a presentation

Trying a new hairstyle

Run for election as a class representative

Singing in a choir

Entering a race

Taking part in a show

Inviting someone you're not really friends with to visit you at your home

Read a text you wrote in front of your class

Going to a party where you don't know many people

Wearing new clothes

Speaking to a stranger

Your fears

Look at the fears you've circled. Do you see similarities between them? Why do you think these things scare you the most? Is it fear of rejection if you reveal your true self? To do wrong? To look ridiculous? To hurt yourself?

The importance of communication
Communication is also a valuable tool for understanding the origins of your fears. Talk about your fears with people you trust, such as your parents, friends or a mental health professional if your fear is disabling. They can help you step back and analyze your fears objectively.

Fear as an opportunity for growth
It's important to remember that fear isn't necessarily a bad thing. In fact, it can be an opportunity for personal growth and development. By facing up to our fears, we learn to surpass ourselves, acquire new skills and strengthen our self-confidence.

By understanding the origin of our fears, we can begin to overcome them and develop our self-confidence. It's important to remember that everyone has their own fears, and that you're not alone in this process. With time, patience and perseverance, you can learn to live without being limited by your fears.

Think of one of your worst moments

Have you ever experienced a major failure? One of those moments you just want to get out of your mind? Coping with failure allows you to grow and gives it less power over you. What has happened to you? How did it make you feel?

If the same thing had happened to a friend

What would you say to comfort him or her? We're always harder on ourselves than on our friends. Look at things as kindly as you would a friend.

How do you deal with failure?

Circle the three methods you use most, or write down others.

Curling up in a
ball under your
comforter

Going for a
long run

Crying on
your pillow

Telling a
friend
about it

Writing in your
secret diary

Watching
a comedy
to cheer
you up

Eating comfort
food

Replaying the
scene 100 times
in your head
imagining how
you could have
changed things

Analyzing
what
happened

Talking to a
trusted adult

Trying to
laugh it
off

Putting it out
of your mind
and moving
on

Listening
to loud
music

Telling yourself
that everyone
makes mistakes

Rehearsing,
practicing,
studying for
next time

Telling
yourself it
could have
been worse

Ideas for overcoming failure

Put things into perspective and play them down. Recall other similar situations, experienced by yourself or someone you know. It's not that bad. No, it's not all anyone talks about.

Be kind to yourself. Everyone makes mistakes, everyone fails. Don't beat yourself up. Life goes on. Things will be better tomorrow.

Change your mind. There's no point dwelling on a mistake. Watch a movie, listen to music, go out with a friend, play sports.

Talk about it. Failure is always painful. Talk about it with caring people, friends, your parents, your favorite teacher, your coach.

Comfort yourself: Use the previous exercise and tell yourself the words you would use to comfort a friend in the same situation.

Analyze: What happened? Why did you fail? Could you have done better? How could you not make the same mistake again? Making a mistake is part of the path, but you must avoid making the same mistake twice.

Some more ideas

Take responsibility: No need to lie to yourself. There was a mistake or mistakes made. You must take responsibility for them, ask for forgiveness if necessary, and study how to make amends if possible.

Make a new plan: Don't dwell on a failure. Prepare for your next success! You were not elected as a class representative? Take the time to establish your future program, more adapted to the needs of your classmates. Find allies. And remember to congratulate the winner!

What I control

My goals

My behavior

Who my friends are

My efforts

How I take
care of myself

The respect and
love I have for
myself

Asking for
help

Learning from
my mistakes

What I don't control

What others
think or say

What I have to
do (homework,
chores)

Past
mistakes

Illness

The
weather

My feelings

What others
do

Think of words of support that you could say to yourself in case of failure or disappointment

"You can always do more than
you think you can."

JOSEPH KESSEL (WRITER)

"You get in life what you have the
courage to ask for."

OPRAH WINFREY (TALK SHOW
HOST, TELEVISION PRODUCER)

Good surprises

Think back to three negative events that happened to you or that you witnessed. Did you observe less negative reactions than you expected? Did people move on more quickly than you expected? Was it as bad as you thought it would be?

1

2

3

Good surprises

Think of three things that you did when you didn't want to and that you finally liked. Or think of three situations that worried you but ended up going better than you expected. It could have been a party you didn't want to go to, a competition you thought you would lose, a dress you were reluctant to wear that earned you a compliment.

1 ____

2 ____

3 ____

Negative thoughts

As you have just seen, much of your fear comes from anticipating failure or rejection when there is no reason for it to happen.

Consider the following quote from René Barjavel, writer: "**To experience misfortune in advance is to suffer it twice**". What do you think about it?

Shutting down negative thoughts

Negative thoughts can be invasive and prevent you from acting by locking you into a perception of yourself that is not true.

Over and over in your head, you may feel that these thoughts are telling the truth, but they're not. Sometimes we don't even realize we're hearing these negative thoughts.

If we're not careful, they can become bad habits and prevent us from realizing our full potential.

What is a negative thought?
It's telling yourself that you'll never be able to do something because you failed once (negative generalization). It's thinking you're useless because you don't understand an exercise (catastrophism). It's believing that you can read people's minds and tell yourself that such and such a person hates you. It's believing that you can predict the future by telling yourself that you're going to fail your test even though you've studied and understood your lessons.

Fighting negative thoughts

The first thing to do to fight a negative thought is to identify it.

Do you often say to yourself or think.
- "I can't"
- "I should..." or "you should..."
- "It's my fault" or "It's his fault"
- "It's not fair"

Other thoughts to get rid of are:
- Catastrophism
- Negative exaggeration
- Believing you can read minds or guess the future
- All or nothing

When you notice a negative thought, you've already come a long way. Now it's time to block it out.

To do this, take a break, go back over your list of successes, think about your favorite places and times, look at the photo that makes you smile (previous chapter), do an activity that makes you feel good.

Shutting down negative thoughts

When you are calm and serene, write down the negative thoughts that sometimes pop into your head:

____

____

____

____

____

____

For each negative thought, rephrase in a more positive and realistic way. Do you really have to generalize? Do you really have to be so hard on yourself? Can you really read other people's thoughts and really predict the future?

____

____

____

____

____

____

Accepting your imperfections

We all have flaws and weaknesses, and that's normal. No one is perfect, and that's what makes each individual unique and special. Learning to accept our imperfections means giving ourselves permission to be ourselves, without judgment or criticism.

The importance of self-acceptance

Self-acceptance is the key to developing strong self-esteem. It means recognizing and embracing all facets of our personality, including our imperfections. By accepting our shortcomings, we free ourselves from the weight of self-criticism.

Changing perspective

Rather than seeing our flaws as obstacles, we can view them as opportunities for growth and learning. Every mistake or failure is an opportunity to learn and improve. By adopting this positive mentality (or growth mindset), we can turn our imperfections into strengths.

Letting go

Perfectionism can be a real obstacle to self-acceptance. When we set ourselves unrealistic standards, we put enormous pressure on ourselves to be perfect. This can lead to a constant sense of failure and dissatisfaction. Learning to let go of perfectionism means giving ourselves permission to be imperfect and to do our best without judging ourselves.

"The first and greatest victory is to conquer yourself."

PLATO (PHILOSOPHER)

"Believe in yourself. Become the kind of person you will be happy to live with for the rest of your life."

GOLDA MEIR (ISRAELIAN STATESWOMAN)

Perfectionism

Do you sometimes feel that what you are doing is not good enough?

How often do you compare yourself to the others?

Do you often dwell on something you've said or done, wishing you could erase it and start over?

Do you feel the pressure of other people's gaze?

Are you constantly trying to please others?

If you answered "yes" to any of these questions then you may be a perfectionist.

Wanting to be perfect all the time is both exhausting and stressful. Striving for excellence is a great quality, but keep in mind that there is no such thing as perfection.

What do you think of the expression: "**Better done than perfect**"? What do you think it means? Can you apply it?

____

____

____

____

____

____

If you could change three things to feel more confident, what would they be?

1

2

3

Are your answers realistic or impractical? Is it reasonable to want to change these three things? If so, how?

Are there areas where you feel pressure to be perfect?

It can be at school, in your family, in your sports or music club, on the Internet.

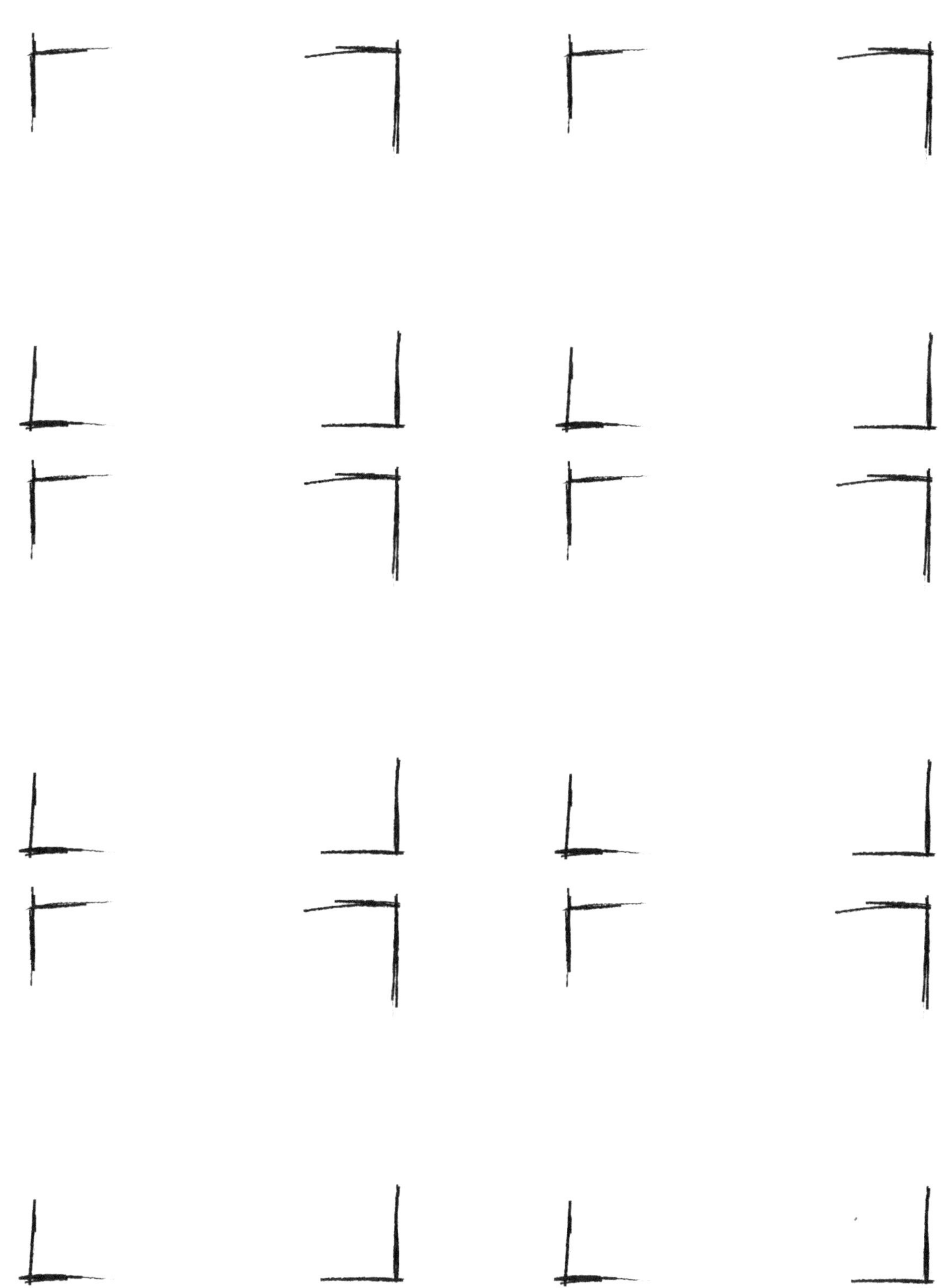

Make a list of things you think you should do but don't really want to do

Why do you think you should do it? What would happen if you didn't?

1

2

3

4

Choose one of the areas where you feel pressure to be perfect

If you could be perfect in this area, what would be your goal?

____

____

____

____

Does this goal seem achievable to you?

____

____

If you find this objective difficult to achieve, have you thought about breaking it down into different steps as suggested in the chapter about your objectives?

____

____

Why or for whom do you think you want to achieve perfection in this field?

____

____

____

Now that you've answered these questions, do you still think you have to (or want to) be perfect in this area?

Learning to say no

Learning to say no is an essential skill for developing self-confidence and establishing healthy boundaries in your relationships with others. Saying no can seem difficult, especially when you want to please others or avoid conflict. However, it's important to remember that saying no is an act of respect towards yourself and helps preserve your emotional and mental well-being.

Why is it important to say no?

Saying no is a way of taking care of yourself and respecting your own needs and limits. It helps you avoid feeling overwhelmed, used or manipulated by others. By saying no, you assert your autonomy and your ability to make decisions that suit you.

How to say no assertively

Saying no assertively means saying "no" clearly, respectfully and without aggression. Here are a few tips to help you:

- **Be clear and direct**: Express your refusal concisely and unambiguously. Use simple sentences and avoid justifying yourself.

- **Stay calm and respectful**: Speak in a calm voice. Show respect for the other person while asserting your position.

- **Use "I" sentences**: For example, say "I'm not available tonight" rather than "You can't count on me tonight".

- **(Possibly) suggest alternatives**: If you can't accept a request, suggest alternatives or compromises that might suit both parties. Don't feel obliged to do so - it's not your job to find solutions to other people's problems, for example.

- **Stay firm**: Don't let yourself be influenced by the other person's attempts at manipulation or persuasion. Stay true to your decision and maintain your limits.

Overcoming the fear of saying no

It's normal to feel apprehensive or afraid when it comes to saying no. However, this fear should not prevent you from asserting yourself and taking care of yourself. Here are a few tips to help you:

- **Identify your fears**: Take some time to think about why you're afraid to say no. Is it the fear of rejection? Is it fear of rejection, disappointment or conflict? Once you've identified your fears, you can start to overcome them.

- **Practice**: Start by saying no to small requests that don't make you too uncomfortable. The more you practice, the more comfortable you'll feel. You can practice in front of a mirror or by asking a family member, for example. This will familiarize you with the words and expressions you want to use, and make you feel more confident when you're faced with a real-life situation.

- **Visualize the positive outcome**: imagine yourself saying no, and feel the satisfaction and relief it brings. Visualizing the positive outcome can help you boost your self-confidence and overcome your fears.

- **Surround yourself with support**: Talk about your difficulties in saying no to people you trust, such as friends and family. They'll be able to support and encourage you.

- **Learn to accept other people's reactions**: Some people may not react favorably to you saying no, especially if they're used to you saying yes. However, remember that you have the right to take care of yourself and set your own limits. Learn to accept other people's reactions without second-guessing yourself.

Comparing yourself to others

Comparing ourselves to others can be an easy trap to fall into. When we constantly compare ourselves to others, we put ourselves in competition and judge ourselves. It's important to remember that each person has his or her own path and challenges. We are all unique and have our own strengths and weaknesses. Focusing on our own personal growth and learning is far more beneficial than comparing ourselves to others.

Being kind to yourself

Self-kindness is an act of self-love and self-compassion. It means speaking to ourselves with kindness and gentleness, as we would to a friend. When we are kind to ourselves, we give ourselves permission to be imperfect, and treat ourselves with respect and understanding. Self-kindness is a powerful tool for building strong self-esteem and lasting self-confidence.

Forgiving yourself 

Do you regret something you did or said and do you often think about it?

____

____

Imagine two years from now, do you think you'll still be thinking about it?

____

____

Knowing that no one is perfect and that everybody makes mistakes, are you willing to forgive yourself?

____

____

What do you think you learned from this experience?

____

____

____

____

Bill Gates, entrepreneur and philanthropist: "It's fine to celebrate success but it is more important to heed the lessons of failure."

Your image

Are there parts of your body that you don't like?
Do you retouch your photos before posting them?

Do you find it hard to believe people who compliment you on your looks or style?

Do you sometimes feel pressure to change your clothes?

If you answered "yes" to any of these questions, you are very concerned about your image. Do you think boys worry as much about their appearance?

To gain self-confidence, build on your strengths and exploit what you like about your appearance. Wear clothes that you feel comfortable in and that make you feel good about yourself. And you're not alone: more than half of secondary school children are dissatisfied with their appearance (46% of girls want a slimmer figure and 27% of boys a stronger one).

Your appearance

Take the list of your female models. Do you think they sometimes feel insecure about their appearance?

____

____

Do you think these women ultimately care more about what they look like than what they do?

____

____

Do you find it easy to find pictures of "normal" women in magazine ads or on TV? Does this make sense to you?

____

____

List below the aspects of your appearance or look that you particularly appreciate:

____

____

____

____

Coco Chanel, fashion designer: "Beauty begins the moment you decide to be yourself".

The place of girls

What does being a girl mean to you?

Do you think that some areas are only for boys or that some activities are more difficult for girls? If so, which ones and why do you think so?

Do you think different attitudes or abilities are expected from girls? List them below:

What do you like about being a girl?

What do you find difficult about being a girl?

Stereotypes

A stereotype is a ready-made opinion, a cliché. It is the characterization of a group (a gender, an origin, a location, an ability, a social background, etc.) based on preconceived expectations and judgments such as "girls are less good at math than boys". Have you ever been exposed to stereotypes?

If so, how did you feel? Did you think it was right?

Do you ever judge someone based on their appearance, their origin, the way they talk, their gender?

Anyone can have prejudices. The important thing is to realize this and think more objectively.

David Augustin de Brueys, theologian: "All prejudices are rooted in ignorance".

Girls have roles and contributions that are just as important, meaningful and valuable as those of boys.

You are in no way limited by society's often narrow expectations of girls. Whether in the academic, professional, artistic or other fields, you have the ability to excel and break down barriers.

You may encounter stereotypes, unfounded expectations based on your gender, your origins (social or geographical), your appearance, the way you speak, etc. But these stereotypes don't define you. But these stereotypes don't define who you are or what you can achieve. You're a unique person with talents, ideas and dreams that have no limits based on criteria that don't relate to your worth.

Stereotypes can be like invisible chains, but remember that you have the power to break them. Never let anyone tell you what you can or can't do. Be proud of who you are, your skills, your aspirations and your voice.

Take your place in society with confidence. Be an inspiration to yourself and others. Embrace every opportunity to grow, learn and make your voice heard. The world needs diverse and rich perspectives, and you're a valuable part of that diversity.

Bullying

Bullying is characterized by the **repeated use of violence**, which can be **verbal** (insults, mockery, criticism), **physical** (threats, blows, unwanted touching) or **psychological** (scornful looks, ostracism, humiliation). There is also appropriation bullying, i.e. **racketeering or extortion**: the victim is forced to give away things that belong to him or her (money, objects, food). This type of violence is perpetrated by one or more people against a victim. It can happen, for example, at school or on social networks (**cyber-bullying**).

Bullying is based on the rejection of difference. The bully or bullies may, for example, make fun of a weaker and/or isolated victim's physical appearance, way of dressing, attitude, disability, stammering or belonging to a particular social or cultural group.

Bullying can have serious consequences for the victim, such as anxiety, depression, low self-esteem and even physical damage. Whatever its supposed reasons, **bullying is never funny, never justified, and must always be reported in order to put a stop to it**.

Albert Camus, writer: "Being different is neither a good nor a bad thing. It simply means that you are brave enough to be yourself."

What to do in response to bullying?

Whether you are a witness or a victim, you are not alone and adults are there to help.

Tell an adult at your school about it

Search for online help*

Tell your parents about it

Tell a friend or friends about it

The important thing is not to act as if nothing has happened, in the hope that it will stop on its own or that it won't happen to you. The bully has to be the one isolated!

Children with the most self-confidence and who are surrounded by others are the least likely to be victims of bullying.

*In the USA: www.stopbullying.gov
 In Canada: www.prevnet.ca
 In the UK: www.gov.uk/bullying-at-school

"All wickedness has its source in weakness."

SENECA (PHILOSOPHER)

"I tend to think that, in general, nastiness is not a proof of intelligence."

RENÉ GOSCINNY (SCRIPTWRITER OF COMICS)

Friends

Friends play an important role in our lives. They are there to support us, listen to us and share moments of joy and sadness with us. But how do we create strong, lasting friendships? How can we find friends who understand and accept us as we are?

Making and keeping friends requires a little risk-taking, trust and communication.

Be yourself
The first step to making friends is to be yourself. Don't try to change who you are to please others. True friends will accept you as you are, with all your qualities and faults. Be authentic and show others who you really are. Don't be afraid to be different, because that's what makes you unique and interesting.

Be open and friendly
To create friendships, it's essential to be open and friendly. Show interest in the people you meet, ask them questions about themselves and listen carefully to their answers. Be attentive and caring. A simple smile or friendly gesture can make all the difference and open the door to beautiful friendships.

Share your interests

A great way to build friendships is to share your interests with others. Whether it's sports, music, video games or reading, find people who share the same passions as you. Join clubs or groups that gather around these activities and you'll meet people who share your interests. This will make it easier for you to bond and build strong friendships.

Be attentive and empathetic

To build strong friendships, it's important to be attentive and empathetic to others. Listen to their needs, emotions and concerns. Show them you care by being present and offering support when needed. Empathy is the key to developing healthy, lasting relationships.

Show respect and tolerance

In any friendship, it's essential to show respect and tolerance. Everyone has their own opinions, beliefs and values, and you need to respect them even if they differ from yours. Avoid hasty judgments and prejudices. Learn to accept differences and value diversity. This will help you build strong, harmonious friendships.

Nurture your friendships

Once you've created friendships, it's time to nurture them. Spend time with your friends, show them you care and share quality time together.

Dealing with conflict

In any friendship, there can be disagreements and conflicts. Deal with them constructively. Avoid aggressive confrontation, preferring open, respectful communication. Express your feelings and concerns in a calm, non-accusatory way. Also listen to your friend's point of view, and together look for ways to resolve the conflict. Friendships that endure hardship and are able to resolve conflict often grow stronger and deeper. You can use the following pages to help you resolve any problems that may arise.

Be patient

Building strong, lasting friendships can take time. Don't be discouraged if you don't make new friends immediately. Be patient and continue to be yourself, open and friendly towards others. Sincere friendships develop gradually and take time to build.

By following these tips, you'll be able to create strong, lasting friendships. Don't forget that friendships are precious and can bring you support, joy, fulfillment throughout your life and boost your self-confidence.

Do you think you're a good friend? Explain why below:

What do you look for in a good friend? It can be useful to make a list of qualities you look for in a friend:

This list will help you understand what you're looking for in a friendship, and the kind of friend you want to be.

Is it easy for you to make new friends? Imagine how you might start talking to a new person.

Good friends

Circle the three qualities or characteristics that are most important to you, or add others.

Makes me laugh

Is sincere

Is trustworthy

Is loyal to me

Understands me

Is nice

Keeps my secrets

Accepts me as I am

Is popular

Supports me

Share my interests

Does not take himself/herself seriously

Makes me feel good

Gives me advice

Encourages me

Makes me want to do new things

Wears nice clothes

Can you identify a **false** friend?

Imagine you have a friend who doesn't have your best interests at heart...

What advice would you give to someone in this situation?

One of the first steps in dealing with a toxic relationship is to establish clear boundaries. It's important to define what you're willing to accept and what you won't tolerate in a relationship. Identify your needs and values and make sure you communicate them clearly to the other person.

Don't be afraid to say no and defend your limits. You deserve to be respected and to feel safe in a relationship. If the other person doesn't respect your limits, it may be necessary to take additional steps to manage the relationship.

Have you ever had a problem with a friend?

How did you address this problem?

____
____
____
____

How did your friend react?   Did you expect this reaction?

____
____
____
____

Do you consider that you have solved the problem or is it still a concern for you?

____
____

How are your relationships now?

____
____
____
____

Would you change the way you approached the problem if you could?

____
____

In case of a problem with a friend

What is the problem?

____

____

____

How do you feel about this problem?

____

____

____

How do you think your friend feels about this problem?

____

____

____

In your opinion, what are the reasons for this problem?

____

____

____

____

How do you feel about this problem?

When faced with a problem with a friend, it's important to express how you feel. A good relationship requires good communication. Using sentences beginning with "I" helps to emphasize your feelings and not be as accusatory as a sentence beginning with "you". Writing also helps you better understand what's going on, what you're feeling, and will help you talk to your friend more calmly.

Write down how you feel below:

)____

____

____

)____

____

____

)____

____

____

)____

____

____

Imagine the conversation you would like to have with this friend

The other day, when (explains what happened)

____

____

____

I felt (describe how you felt, use the previous page)

____

____

____

I know that I (take on your share of responsibility, if necessary)

____

____

Can you tell me if you did it on purpose? (give him the opportunity to explain)

____

Maybe next time we could (find a compromise)

____

____

____

It's up to you now !

Here's the perfect tool if you're having a conflict with someone, or just need to express how you feel.

Example: I feel irritated **when** you enter my room without knocking **because** it tells me you don't respect my privacy. **I need you to** knock and ask before entering.

Have you talked to your friend?

How did it go? Were you able to make her/him understand how you felt?

____

____

____

____

____

____

____

What would you do differently another time?

____

____

____

____

____

____

____

Think about the friend who seems to have the most confidence in him/her. How does this confidence express itself?

1. ___________________________________

2. ___________________________________

3. ___________________________________

Do you think you can imitate these behaviors without it feeling completely artificial or awkward? Sometimes, building self-confidence also starts with appearing more confident than you really are. Fake it till you make it !

"Life is a challenge, we must take it."

MOTHER TERESA (NOBEL PEACE
PRIZE, MISSIONARY)

"Do not bring people in your life who weigh you down. And trust your instincts."

MICHELLE OBAMA (AMERICAN
FIRST LADY)

As a conclusion

As you have seen throughout the pages, self-confidence is fueled by life-long experiences.

It is normal to be afraid, to doubt, to make mistakes, to fail. But this should never stop you from trying, starting over, moving forward.

The more you get to know and appreciate yourself, the more you will accept yourself as you are. The more you take risks and act, the more you will gain self-confidence.

Having a full and rewarding life requires courage. In the words of South African statesman Nelson Mandela, "courage is not the absence of fear, but the ability to overcome that which is frightening". So it is okay to be scared, but it shouldn't stop you from acting and living your life to the fullest.

You can do it, believe in yourself!

My takeaways

1 ________________________________

____

____

2 ________________________________

____

____

3 ________________________________

____

____

4 ________________________________

____

____

5 ________________________________

____

____

6 ________________________________

____

____

What I will do

1.

2.

3.

4.

5.

6.